GIRL + DOG INVESTIGATE:

THE WOUND

A TRUE FIELD REPORT

by

Girl

with *Special Appearances* by

dog

Girl+dog Investigate: The Wound

Dark Cave Press, Australia

National Library of Australia

Cataloging-in-Publication entry

ISBN-13: 978-0-6484036-4-7 (paperback)

For all

and none

CONTENTS

Girl: dog, can we know the wound?

dog: *raises paw, pointing north to walk with people*

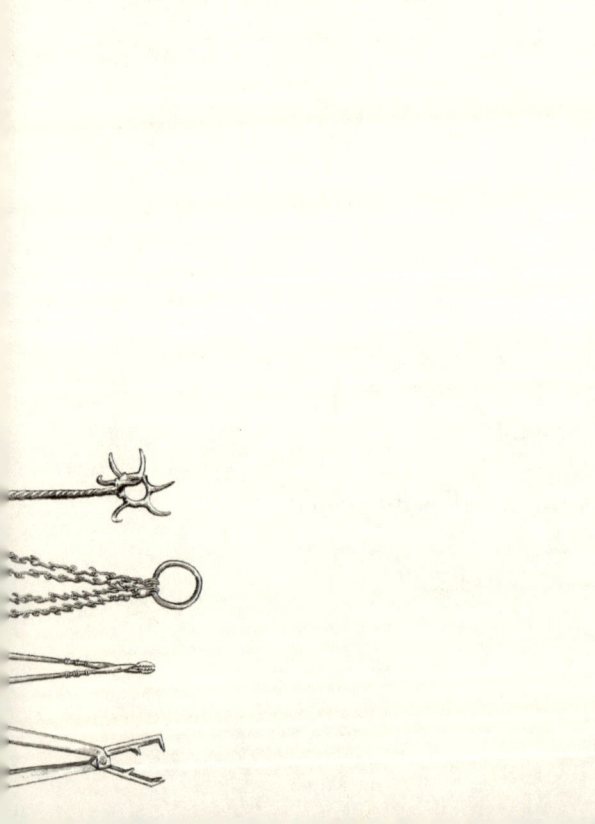

PROLOGUE

I'm figuring out a problem with dog. From eye's corner I glimpse the flit of solution. dog was bred for seeing the invisible. I ask dog, How do I get to Dublin? dog says, Go to Berlin.

The Pyrrhonists figured out, to solve a problem, they needed to be relaxed; they called the state *ataraxia*. They made ataraxia their goal but could never get there.

They took long walks with their dogs. Two shadows on red soil tailing two thinkers over the headlands marking the Ionian Sea.

"As if by chance," said Sextus. He never understood how walking with the dog was passage and process. If you try to explain this, it will disappear.

II

TALKING WITH STRANGERS

listening Canberra

wound hearing

Stranger: "one who has stopped talking"

[extra] – in addition to what
is usual or expected

Girl + dog wish to express their gratitude, thanks, and humility for all the participants in this deep study of culture and practice. Where possible, the actual words of participants, as given at the time, have been used. Names and places have been altered to protect the brave and the stupid alike.

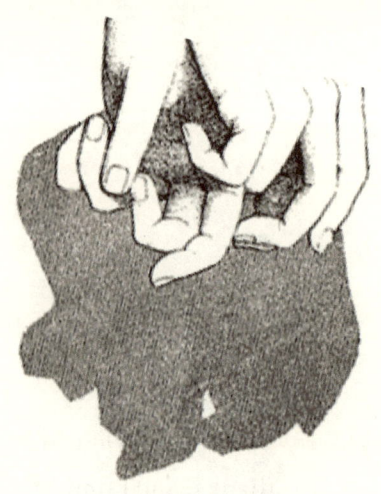

Girl: dog, do you think the poems we collect will make a book?

dog: *knits brow*

Girl: I'm not sure either.

dog: *rests muzzle on lap*

Girl: I agree. Let's give it a bash.

If you are a fieldworker, like us, and happen to overhear wound talk, please add your research to the archive by sending your notes to:

PO Box 54

Dickson ACT 2602

Australia

III

KINSHIP AND SO-CIAL STRUCTURE

An essential prerequisite for the study of any community is a sufficient knowledge of its social structure

Notes & Queries on Anthropology, 6th Ed., RAI

Gemeinschaft: "knowledge, news, tidings"

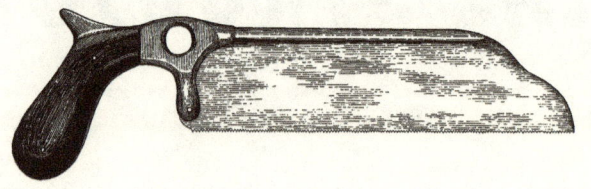

You want to know what I endure?

People who don't say hello.

People who only say goodbye.

People who can't find north.

People whose legs are held on with clips.

People who are birds.

People that should be shot.

Sean *(17) Giralang*

Told me he'd picked up a hand from the table and placed it on the trolley. Wheeled to the next occasional table; gathered more wine-glasses and hands. The glasses, he knew, belonged to the Centre. But the hands, he felt them, each for a taste, seeing if they were his or belonged, in that dead-feel way, to another other.

Gary *(32) Belconnen Arts Centre*

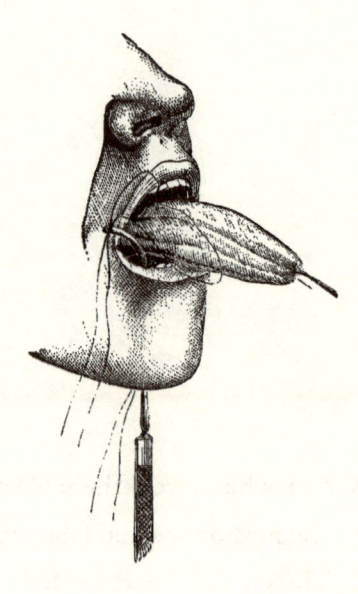

I had this boyfriend; bled to press my brow hard to his

our teeth gritted, splitted

I poured my garbage into him and rated

what it is we're dealing with here

If he didn't run

he's good enough to love for

a while and some

Taylah *(29) private residence in Greenway*

I know the memory of Derek is a kind of Derek. A kind of
new me and him. I think of him, love him, talk to him
and he is alive. But really, he's dead. But he's
not dead. He's just not alive anymore.
If I could hear his voice. Hear him moan
about the Labor party. Get the irits.
If I could see him look at me with hunger and regret and
ache. From then, as now, I know his tongue. His crotchety ways.
I miss his sour body. That one thing I can't
have. His beefy arms to cuddle. And how making
him laugh felt like setting free birds.

Beryl *(52) Junior Guide Leader, Weston Creek Unit*

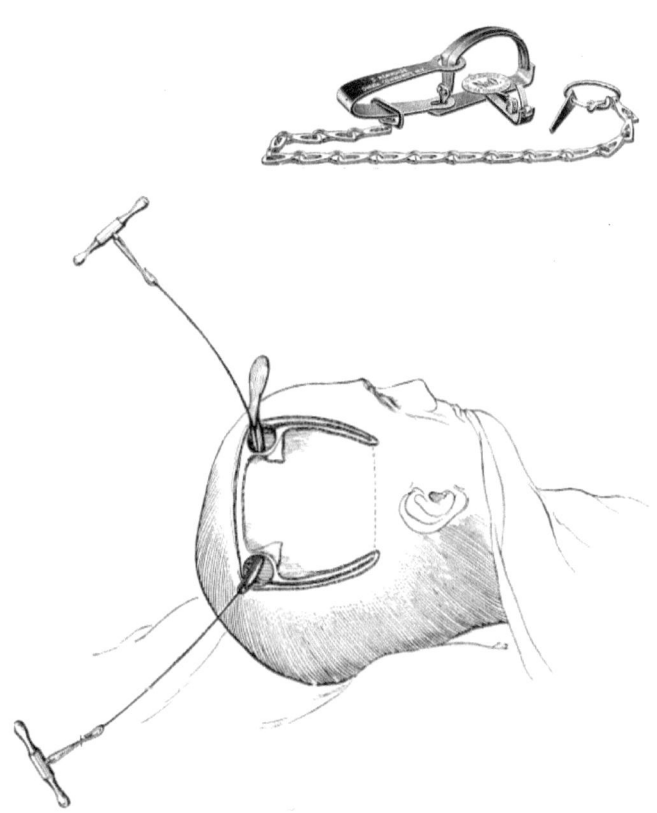

If you don't want people to know you killed him always remember to ask how he died. If I tell you my boyfriend died, and you have been shagging him but he broke it off at the club's Wednesday all-you-can-eat seafood buffet, remember to ask me how he died. I'll tell you he was stabbed with a lobster claw. Then we can keep shopping for your barrette fascinator to match the sapphire cone heels.

Tiphanny *(19) CIT campus*

There's something I want you to know, she told me.

To be real is to be loved. Nothing is ugly. Especially the ugly, she said.

You are ugly, she told me, I like that and I take you as mine; make solemn affirmation while I read you the rules.

These are the rules, she read to me; Each day you will confess, admit passage into you, and render habitual obedience. Be by my feet and between my legs. If ill befalls me, that blemish rests on you.

In return, she told me, I will let you love me.

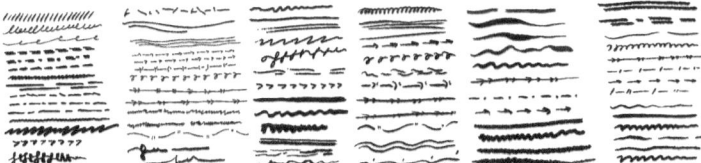

Danielle *(32) Transgrid Substation, Parkwood Road*

Girl: Can you hear what I hear dog?

dog: *nods*

Girl: A pattern is energy.

dog: *nods*

Girl: Let's keep walking.

dog: *steps forward*

IV

TOOLS &
TECHNOLOGY

*The limb to be amputated is not to be held by the assistant
in the manner described and usually shown in books:
one hand ought not to be above the knee,
but below and by the side of it,
the other grasping the calf, so that the limb
may be duly supported, and drawn inward or outward,
in the opposite direction to the saw,
as it divides the last layers of the bone*

G. J. Guthrie, 1862. Commentaries on the Surgery of the War in Portugal, Spain,
France, and the Netherlands. Philadelphia: Lippincott and Co.

It wasn't science in the end, it was the snake milkers; the art of gentle but firm. That was where the real knowledge came from.

Labs had been doing the dirty on mice for a century; mice are small and don't bite back.

They found the hormone system for why some people see black as one colour while others (like you and me) see the dark, the midnight, the pure sad, big onyx, eye-hole coal, red-back black, and ebony pearl.

But it wasn't the white coats and big bucks that found it. It was the hands people, starting with the snake milkers.

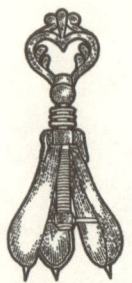

See, you've got to touch. That's the most important thing. When you touch, well... the systems, they start talking. All the systems have their own dialect; unique to every flesh and spirit.

Look at your muscle system. It talks through mocking; it's not afraid of you. That's why, when you work your bicep you can lay a free hand on and say, I know you're not afraid of me but I'm going to hurt you now. That's what I learnt from the snake milkers.

Press your hand on. Squeeze even like you're testing fruit. Go for the hurting places. Say, I'm going to hurt you now. This activates the syrup system. You'll start to thicken and melt all at once.

Hurt and touch, and *say* you're going to because it takes you deeper. That's how they get the snakes to bleed milk.

Sawork *(48) Shine Dome, Acton*

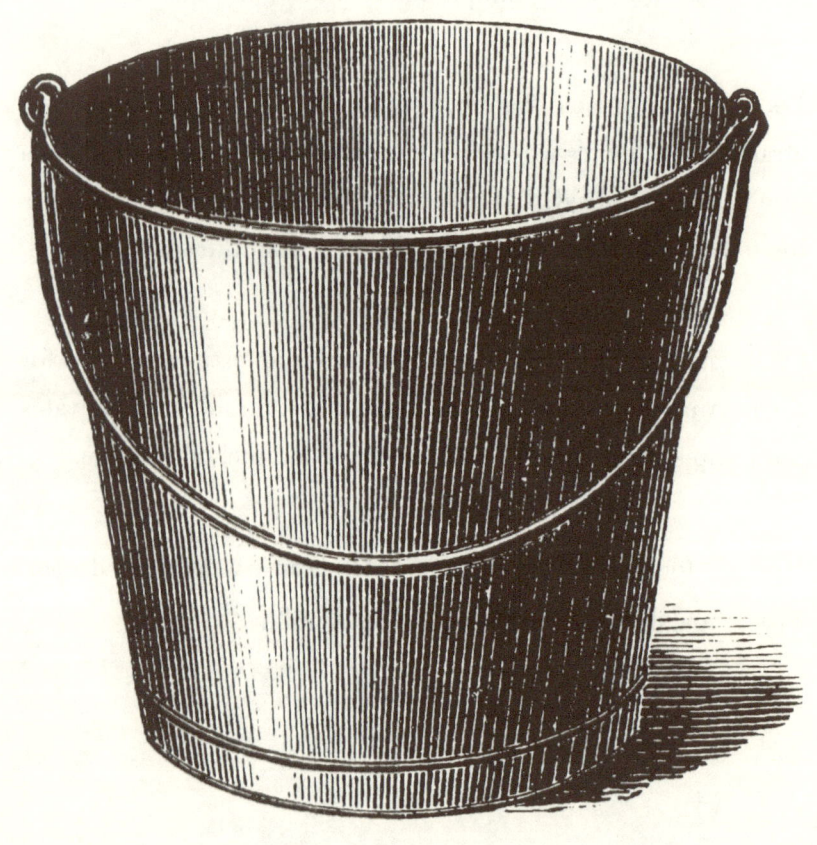

Curly *(34) The boring part of Wanniassa*

I like

big buckets.

You want my opinion? Firstly, if you're aiming to take over the world, don't try for it on the first day of your period.

Doreen *(53) first car was a Celica, Grace*

Girl: It's a quiet law of fieldwork to not interfere, dog.

dog: *listens*

Girl: We're supposed to observe and perhaps ask for more when we feel near the threshold of knowledge.

dog: *small bark*

Girl: You like that we gather and sometimes we hunt?

dog: *blinks*

Girl: We put pieces together, side-by-side, dog. We see the same thing in different ways, and we have discovered our first pattern — a pattern of the wound.

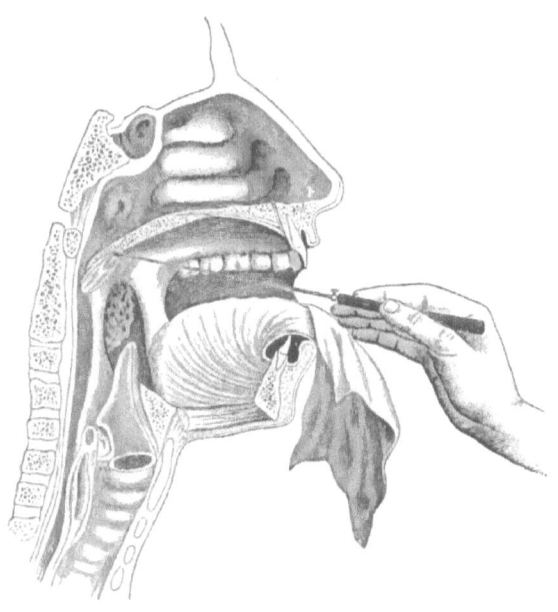

V

RITES & RITUALS

speak

act

(1)a. fire (2)b. smoke (3)c. ascend (4)d. purify

Some things are up to me and others not.
Epictetus

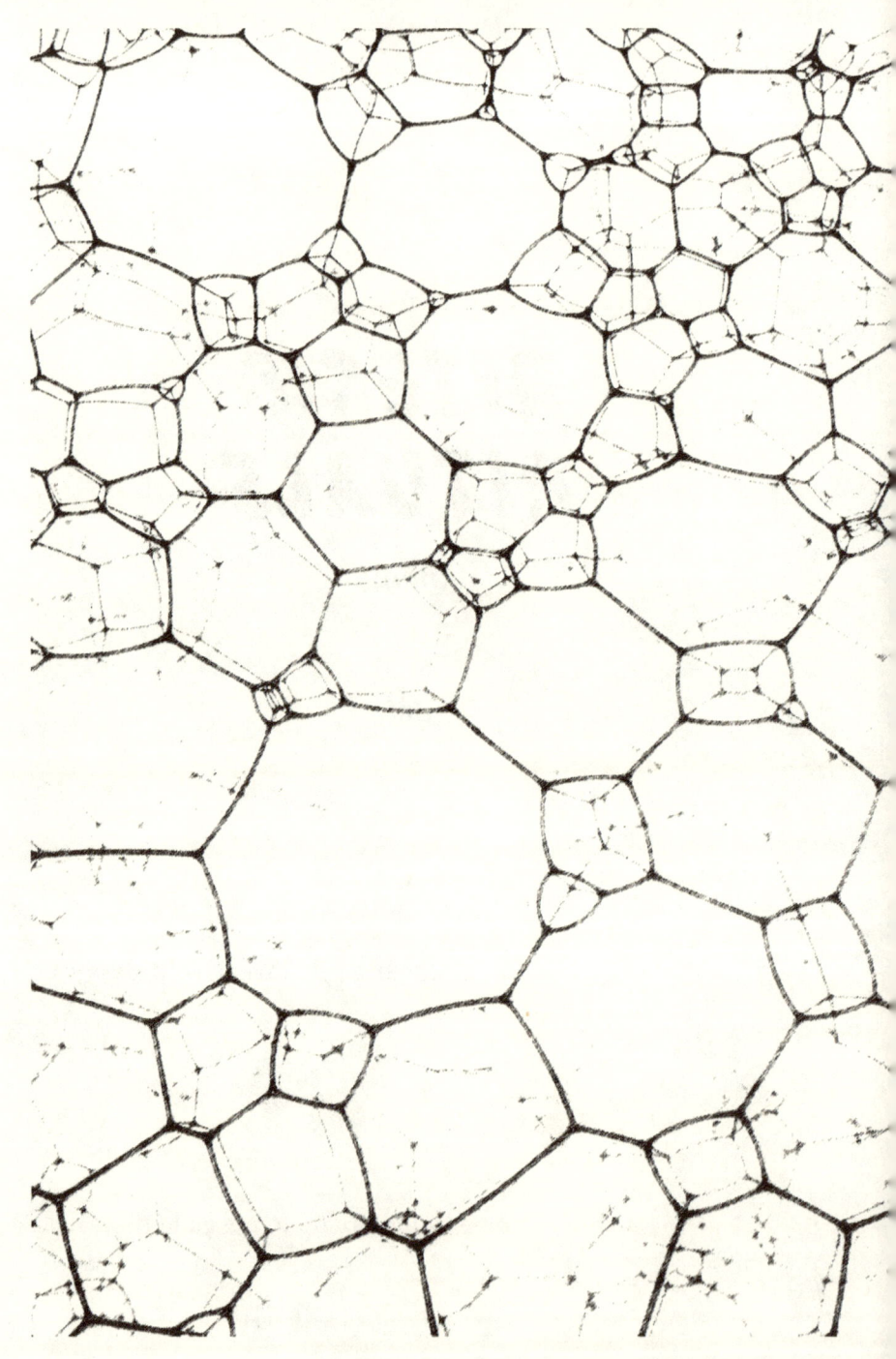

We call them 'grandmother's ashes' but they were not ashes that belonged to her. They were her dead body after it went through a process of breaking atomic bonds.

Atomic bonds are the least important of all the bonds.

Jess *(22) Voyager Park, Red Hill*

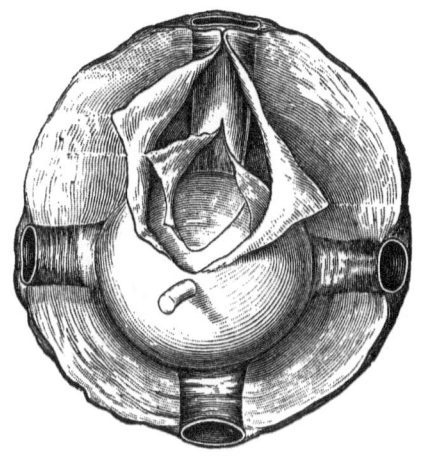

You tell me. You tell me which you think are true,

a. The zebra proves the horse.

b. The aversion proves the pain.

c. If it looks like a duck, it looks like a duck.

Timothy *(16) Straddling footpath cracks in Braddon*

Does this hurt?

–Yes.

Where?

–Here.

In your torso?

–It hurts in the chair.

The heated poker on your hip hurts in the chair?

–Yes.

Which chair?

–The chair near the door.

What about this? I'm pushing a pin into your thigh; does
        that hurt in the chair?

–I cannot feel it in the chair.

I'm pushing deeper, to the pinhead. Anything?

–I feel it in the rug.

The door-mat?

–The Persian rug, next door. The one in their living room.

Is the rug averse, unwanting?

–The rug says it is an experience.

One final calibration. Talk if you can. I'm clamping your
lower lip with the vice.

–It is felt.

Tighter.

–It is in the orphan.

What does the orphan say?

–It's a strange tongue but it sounds like pain.

Can you feel it too?

–Yes. Me and the orphan.

Do they deserve?

–Someone says they do.

Do you?

–The orphan thinks so.

Anonymous *Telephone booth, Oaks Estate*

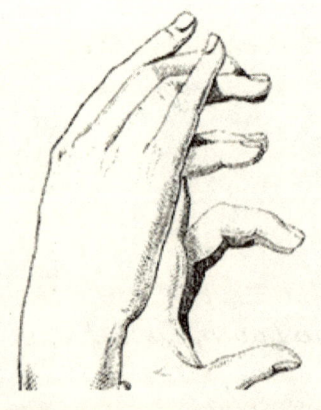

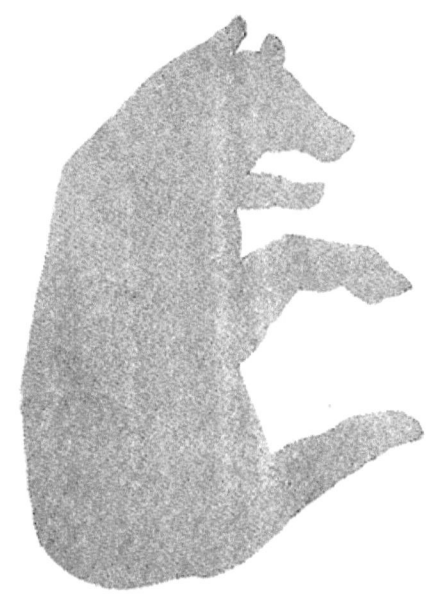

Don't wait. Make inquiries.

Go see *that* man about *that* dog.

Fray *(61) Scratched steel sink,*
Molonglo Reach Toilets

Girl: dog, you know some people think writing *is* fieldwork?

dog: *nods*

Girl: How can we tell them our field notes are only ever in draft?

dog: *thinks*

Girl: Can we tell them about other ethnographies? Good ones?

dog: *shakes head*

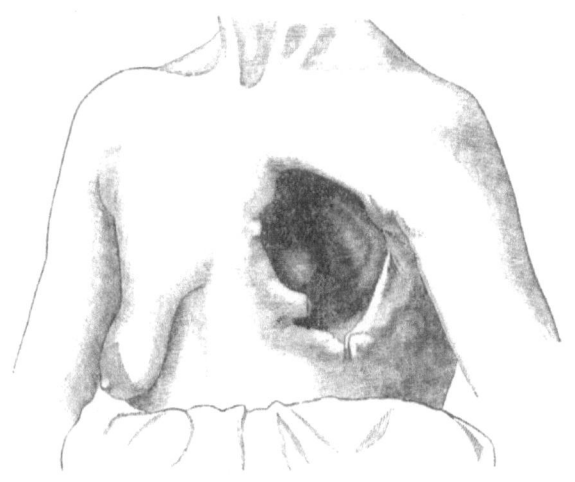

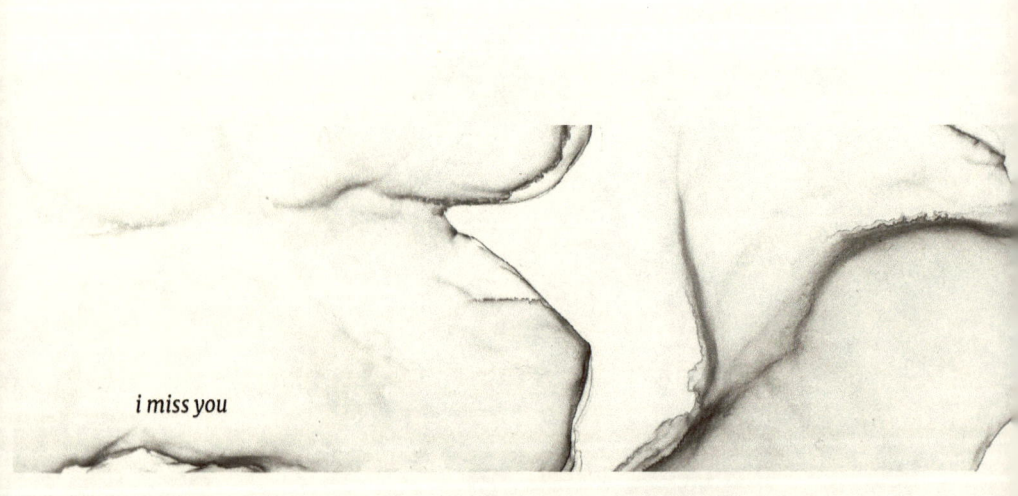

i miss you

VI

SHAPE-SHIFT-ERS, WITCHES, & OUR DEAD

What are the Diseases in general that belong to Sur-
gery? They are Tumours, Impostumes, Wounds, Ulcers,
Fractures, Dislocations, and generally all sorts of Dis-
tempers whereto Manual Operations may be applyed.

M. le Clerc, 1696. The Compleat Surgeon: Or, The whole
Art of Surgery explain'd in a most familiar Method.

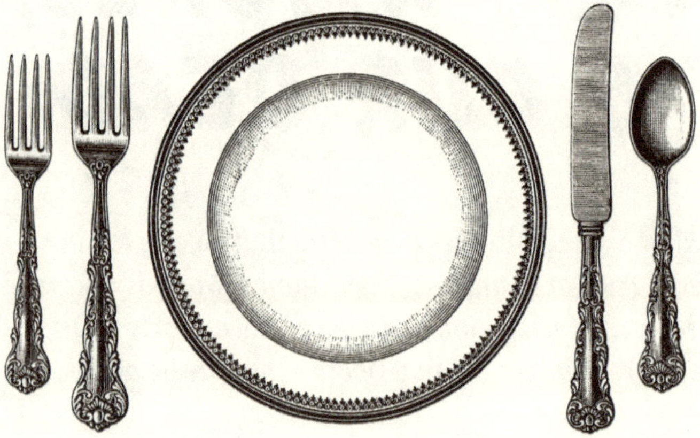

I was stopped running up the mountain. Then I stopped. Then I died. I was man-slaughtered by a boy and another boy and I am a boy. Then I died. The teacher pressed on me. Chest chest chest chest. Pinch-mouth. Pause. Chest chest chest chest. Then I died. There are harder things. People die everyday. I got to die once, on the mountain. I'll stay died until I am dead.

Soul *(17) Mt Ainslie*

We took the copper from her eyes and fed it to the machinery. It ran three days over troughs and gullies. She tap taps the white-ball at door jambs, sizing up the weight of chains and the heights of water. She gets a nice benefit from the Office now she's blind to the underground. And she sells a lot of pity papers to passers-by in peak hour. Alms Almanac and Codswallop. She pulls a lot of pity shags too but she did that before the eyes. Difference being, back then, we couldn't frame her as broke for benefit. When time comes for an Institution, we'll see her right.

Rob *(56)* & **Denise** *(55) dirt track, Stromlo*

Kept touching the spot. Madonna once. Held the spine to the window and squinted. Stephen King signed before. Axel Rose wore this t-shirt. My sweat to his sweat. We're almost lovers. Andrea rang. Saw a Hemsworth at the airport. He was ordering coffee. Does he take sugar? Should we take sugar? If we sip now then we are.

Eftarbordis Sisters *(47 & 49) Gus' cafe*

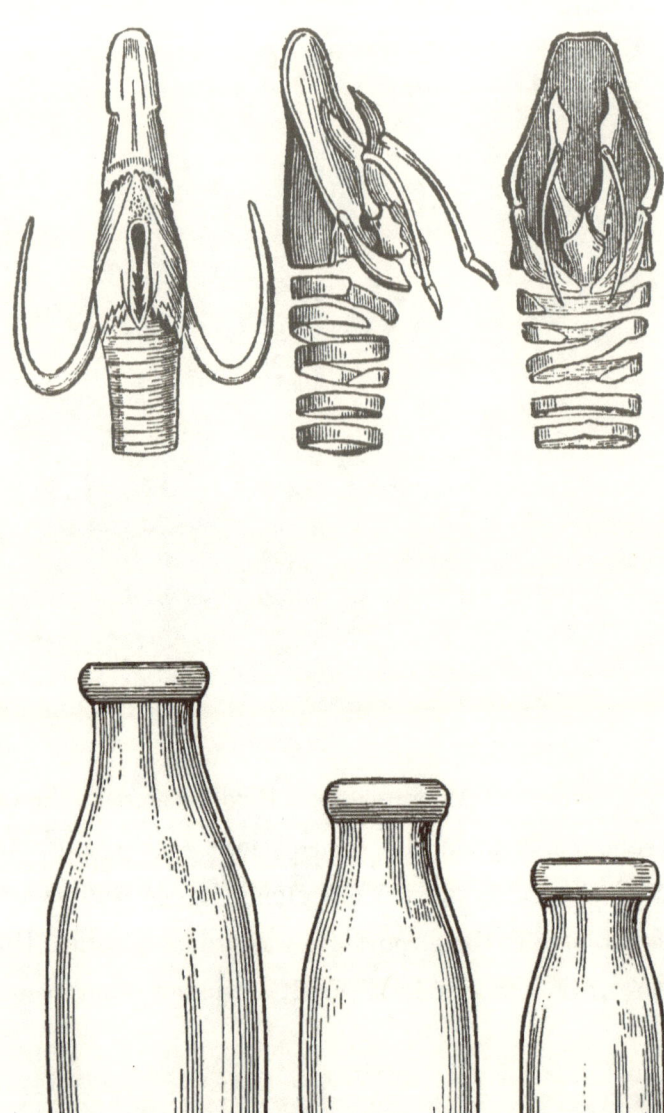

I used to think my old house made me sick. I get the thoughts here, in the new house.

It's houses make you sick.

Cars make you sick.

Nickel makes you sick.

Nylon. Sick.

No mug's safe.

Hug your kids. Hope the end drops quick.

Angela *(46) Watson*

When you get your diagnosis, you're gone.

I hit myself. A fist to my jaw. Dead easy to put violence in. I sum zero.

Questions will come. And come. Lock them away. Be empty and bruise your no more self.

Piss off to everything. To me. The questions. To that sickness who skews your rope to the future.

You'll think you did enough: paid dues, gave penance. Atoned. I take a fist to my stomach. It is not enough.

Rey *(33) Old Tralee Track*

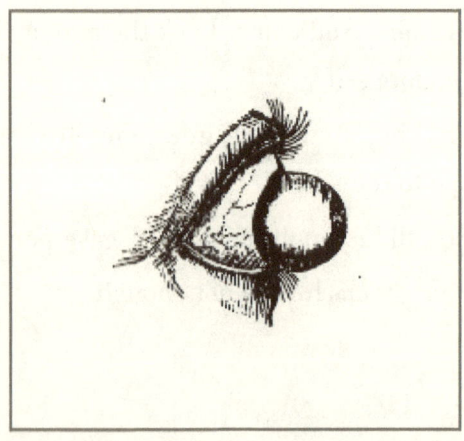

Girl: What is the wound dog?

dog: *looks to the sky*

Girl: I can see, dog, the wound hurts.

dog: *tips muzzle in a nod*

Girl: What do they make that mean?

dog: *blinks*

Girl: Yeah, it depends.

dog and Girl: *gaze eye to eye*

VII

MYTH & STORY

"The wound must be carried deep between the mus-
cles till the prostate can be felt, when searching for
the staff, and fixing it properly, if it has slipped, you
must turn the edge of your knife upwards, and cut the
whole length of the gland from within outwards."

C. Aston Key, 1824. A Short Treatise on the Sec-
tion of the Prostate Gland in Lithotomy

real actual valid true fact fiction

from within outwards

A blow to the head that we've forgotten. I have forgotten but I know it happened. I feel it by means of body.

They say things about me. They chart my desires. They tell me I will die. I say, In what case is that actually true?

Melanie *(83) Place of worship, Melba*

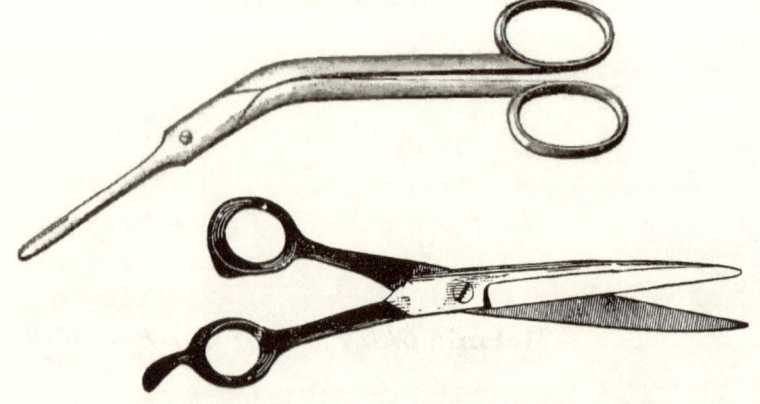

Things can be removed from your brain. Pieces of brain. Types of trauma. Memories. Light bulbs. Copper wire. Microchips. Or so they say.

Stuff grows in your brain. More brain. Tumours and tubers. Wicked ideas. Oaks, beech. Cockroach infestations. That's science.

Objects furrow homes in your brain. Cabins. Hotels. Beaver dams. Nests. Secondary rehabilitated landscapes following bushfire.

An inviting home, warmth hearth, some PJ Wodehouse, and the objects call upon your brain. Puppets. Shells. Food. Shockwaves. Clocks.

Because if pain is a mental object.

What could I possibly say to you that eases or understands? If pain is a mental object then we are already walking amiss. We are walking wounds.

Vincent *(72) Yarralumla Nursery*

Ruth *(56)* **& Scott** *(56) Casuarina Sands*

Viscum crawled into our veins

Wriggled into our brain

And we started to see the world in double

We saw the sun and we saw the object, The Sun

We saw the sun as he scalds, heats, lights

We saw the other sun too

The sun on flags, in stories

Husband to the moon, softening wax of wings

We made our object, The Body

We cut into bodies to find The Body

Etchings of guts and snail shell ears

The Body coheres

With The Body came concussion

We forgot The Body was prototype

We put our bodies in cardboard coffins

We buried them on islands

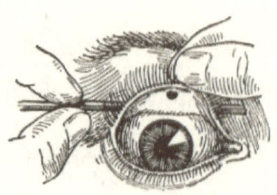

It's vice and de-vice. Each day is made of spent minutes. Spending means they fly from your body and whirl into the heavens. A minute watering the dead spider plant. Then whirring past your nose, your disbursements. Eighty-two minutes staring through the slots of your device. Time flies and you feel heavier, closer to the plot. Nearer the iron skillet. Rag around the handle to save your skin. Skint means you be broke; it's the was of skin. Time's up.

Fran *(approx. 24) cabin of her 18 wheeler,*
Hughie Edwards VC Rest Area, Majura

About me? You want to know how I became a filler?

Time ago, I tried. I used to care. All that's left is the wake of loss.

And sorrowing. I'm not even that any more. Scarcely sad.

I cried into a bucket. The first tears rang out on the echoing steel base. It filled. Then the laundry tub.

Alive and I cry. Astonishing pain fills my skin bag. So much.

Olivia *(26) Throsby*

We weren't equal friends. She was better at stuff than me. She was sort of miraculous.

Everybody said the only reason Josh was still alive was because Lucia had got him off horse. I thought that meant something about love.

If I went to a party at their house in Narrabundah I'd try to sit near Adam. He was the keyboard player and sort of shy. He never minded if I sat quietly rather than talked.

Josh talked a lot. He was always two steps away from being made dead somehow. Lucia got tired of it and moved out.

Josh got back on. The parties weren't parties anymore.

I visited Lucia in her new flat in Cook. She had pot-plants.

There's people in the world who love each other like they're the ones who invented love. They were from that. And I liked being near them.

Glen *(61) HMAS Harman*

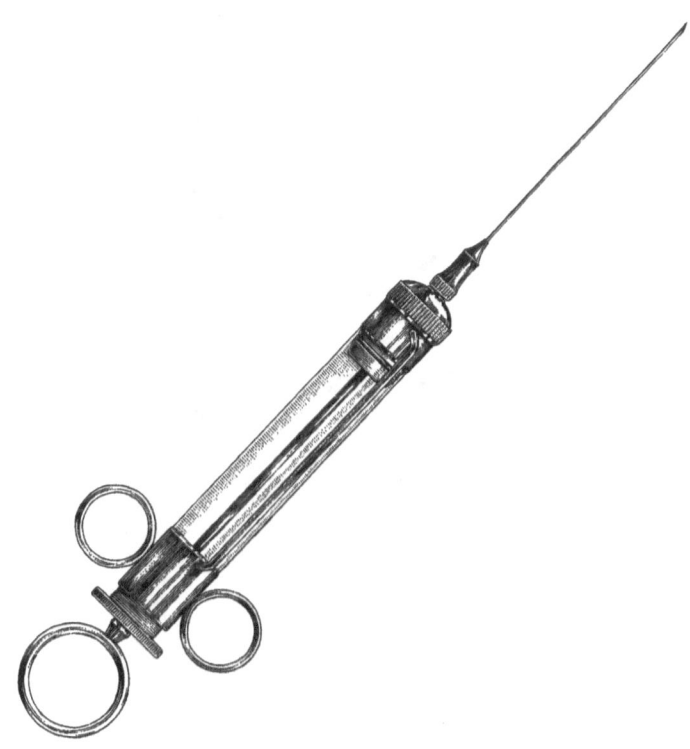

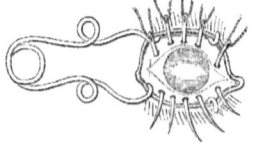

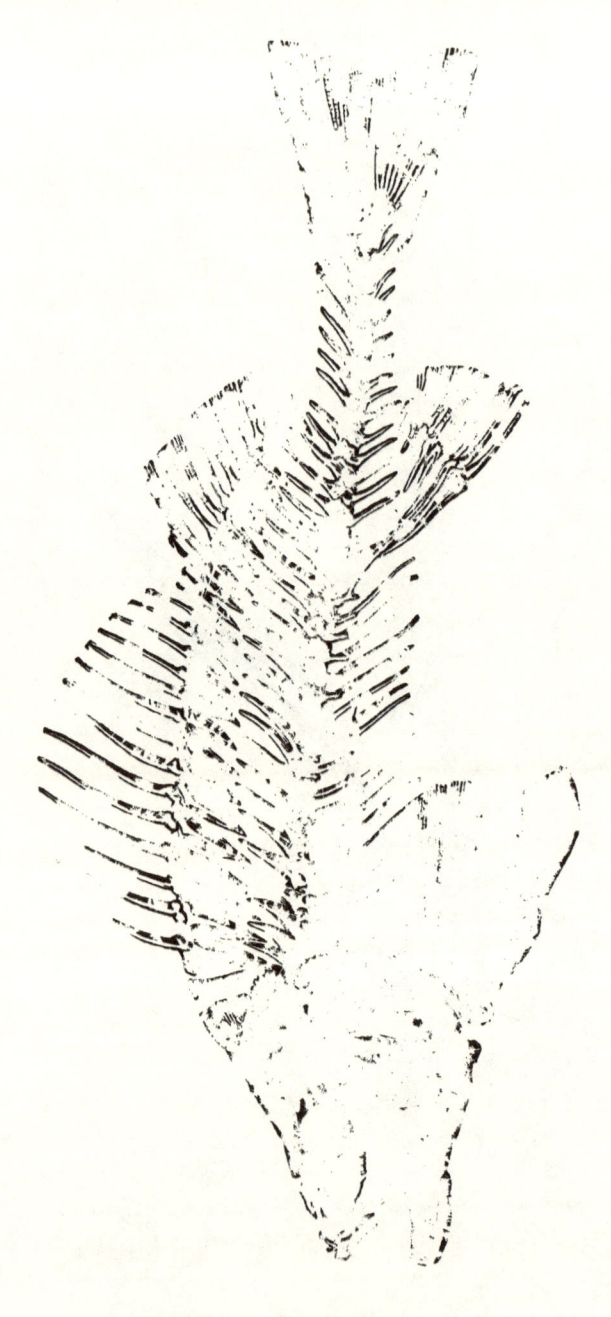

In the morning meeting

I studied close-ups of spider's faces. At first, the faces were unsettling. Differences announced themselves. Staying with a face, intelligence in the eyes came forth. Their whiskers grew to all spaces. Ability to see the mouth came and went like duck-rabbit. An octopus or cuttlefish showed through. A petticoat seam beneath magnificent silk skirts. Unsettled prickles smoothed into a radiance of affection and wonder. The faces in the meeting are boxed. They seemed small for full humans. I saw the faces of spiders beneath their bored, tired fronts.

Cyrus *(29) Undisclosed government agency*

Night-sticks steal your dignity. Marriage white-ants your ilk. Nothing can take your pain from you. Seek your pain.

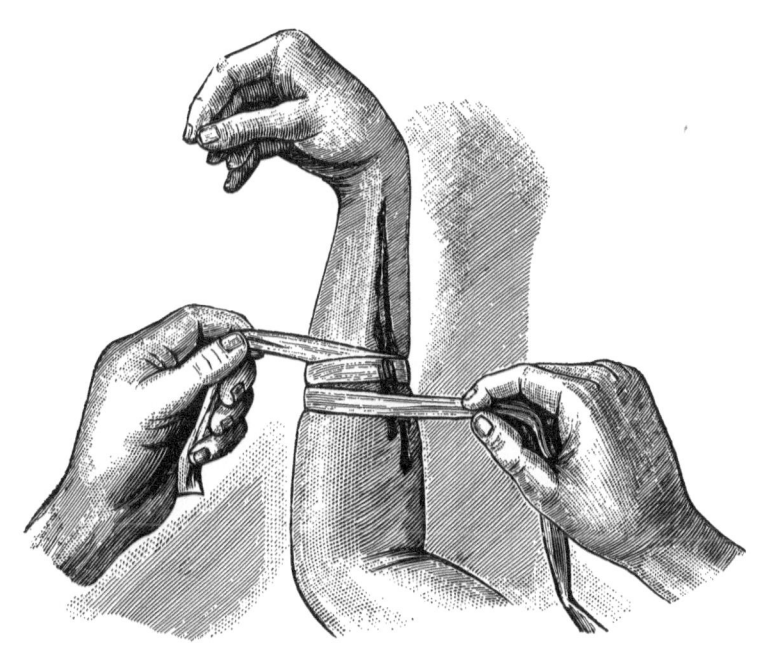

Extract from letter of **Judith** *(82) Woden Cemetery*
to **Mary** *(78) Woden Hospital*

Girl: What happens when a dog dies?

dog: *tilts head*

Girl: Are you scared?

dog: ~

Girl: I'll be with you. I promise.

VIII
TEXTS CON-SULTED

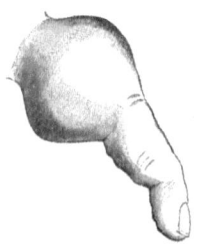

Bechstein, J. M. 1812. *The Natural History of Cage Birds*. London: Groombridge & Sons.

Kirk, J. 1904. *Papers on Health*. London: Hamilton Kent & Co.

Pepper, W. and L. Starr (Eds.) 1885. *A System of Practical Medicine*. Philadelphia: Lea Brothers & Co.

Rawling, L. B. 1912. *The Surgery of the Skull and Brain*. London: Oxford University Press.

Winslow, K. 1907. *The Home Medical Library*. New York: The Review of Reviews Co.

IX

NOTES & SKETCHES

Use this space to collect your fieldwork notes.

www.ingramcontent.com/pod-product-compliance
Lightning Source LLC
Chambersburg PA
CBHW030417120726
47904CB00007B/2312